BULLDOZER
Helps Out

BULLDOZER

Candace Fleming

Helps Out

and Eric Rohmann

A
atheneum

A Caitlyn Dlouhy Book
ATHENEUM BOOKS FOR YOUNG READERS
New York   London   Toronto   Sydney   New Delhi

The construction site bustled.

Cement Mixer was stirring . . .
stirring . . .
stirring.

Crane Truck was lifting ...
lifting ...
lifting.

Digger Truck was scooping ...
scooping ...
scooping.

And Bulldozer was—
   "Watching…watching…watching,"
   he said with a sigh.

Puffing some smoke from his stack,
he bumped to where the other trucks worked.

"*I can help*," he exclaimed.
He raised his blade hopefully.

"You're too little," rumbled Dump Truck. "You'll get hurt."

"Building skyscrapers is a rough, tough job," clattered Cement Mixer.

"For rough, tough trucks," rattled Digger.

Bulldozer
turned
away.

The big trucks looked at one another.

"But maybe . . .," clanged Crane.

"See over there?" Crane pointed. "That needs to be cleared and flattened."

"I can do it! I can do it!" cried Bulldozer.

"So what are you waiting for, kid?" grumbled Roller Truck.

"Hooray!" squealed Bulldozer.
Honking his horn, he zoomed—*bump-vroom*—
to *his* work site.
Once there, he revved his motor.
He lowered his blade.

"Cha-

He sat, smoke puffing from his stack, for a moment.

Then he gave the pile
a little nudge.
Then a second.
Then a third.

And when he'd gotten it just right,
he hunkered down,
hushed and watchful.
His motor hummed,
soft as a lullaby.

Hours passed.

At last—
the other trucks bumped
to where Bulldozer was working.

He hadn't done a single thing they'd asked!

"*I thought he was big enough,*" boomed Digger.
"*I thought he was rough enough,*" rattled Scraper.
"*I thought he was tough enough,*" clattered Grader.

"Move out of the way, kid," roared Roller.
"I'll fix that in no time flat."

But Bulldozer wouldn't budge.
Instead, he whispered, "Shhh!"

"How rude," belched Cement Mixer.

SHHH!

"Behave yourself," rattled Scraper.

SHHHH!

"You mind Roller Truck this minute," clanged Crane.

SHHHHH!

Then—

Above the banging...
rattling...
rumbling...
floated a tiny sweet sound.

The trucks quieted. And in the silence,
a chorus of gentle mews rose into the air.

"Is that what I think it is?" boomed Digger.

Bulldozer raised his blade.
He moved aside.

"They're pretty cute, kid," said Dump Truck.

"But taking care of babies?
Now *that*'s a rough, tough job."

"I can do it! I can do it!" cried Bulldozer.

The big trucks looked at one another again.
"We believe you can," clanged Crane.

And he did.

For Caitlyn and Ann, noble foremen of our construction site
—C. F. and E. R.

atheneum

ATHENEUM BOOKS FOR YOUNG READERS
An imprint of Simon & Schuster Children's Publishing Division
1230 Avenue of the Americas, New York, New York 10020
Text copyright © 2017 by Candace Fleming
Illustrations copyright © 2017 by Eric Rohmann
ATHENEUM BOOKS FOR YOUNG READERS is a registered
trademark of Simon & Schuster, Inc.
Atheneum logo is a trademark of Simon & Schuster, Inc.
For information about special discounts for bulk purchases, please
contact Simon & Schuster Special Sales at 1-866-506-1949 or
business@simonandschuster.com.
The Simon & Schuster Speakers Bureau can bring authors to your
live event. For more information or to book an event, contact the
Simon & Schuster Speakers Bureau at 1-866-248-3049 or visit our
website at www.simonspeakers.com.
Book design by Ann Bobco
The text for this book was set in Futura BT.
The illustrations for this book were made using relief (block) prints.
Three plates were used for each image. The first two plates were
printed in multiple colors, using a relief printmaking process called
"reduction printing." The last plate was the "key" image, which was
printed in black over the color.
Manufactured in China
0217 SCP
First Edition
10 9 8 7 6 5 4 3 2 1
CIP data for this book is available from the Library of Congress.
ISBN 978-1-4814-5894-8
ISBN 978-1-4814-5895-5 (eBook)